Toffee and Pie

PIPPA GOODHART

ILLUSTRATED BY
PAUL HOWARD

WALKER
BOOKS

For everyone at Norton Primary School,
with love
P.G.

For Chris, Stan, Alf and Yoda,
with love
P.H.

First published 2008 by Walker Books Ltd
87 Vauxhall Walk, London SE11 5HJ

4 6 8 10 9 7 5

Text © 2008 Pippa Goodhart
Illustrations © 2008 Paul Howard

The right of Pippa Goodhart and Paul Howard to be identified as author
and illustrator respectively of this work has been asserted by them in
accordance with the Copyright, Designs and Patents Act 1988

This book has been typeset in Bembo Educational
and Cochin-BoldItalic

Printed and bound in China

British Library Cataloguing in Publication Data:
a catalogue record for this book is available from the British Library

ISBN 978-1-4063-1136-5

www.walker.co.uk

A New Place

*J*ohn lived in a silver trailer with his mum, dad, brother and sister. They had an old cart too, which Dad used for collecting things. It was pulled along by a pony called Pie.

Pie was a black and white cob with feathery tufts above her heels, and a mane and tail that blew out like flags in a breeze when she trotted along.

John's family stopped in a new place by a busy road.

"School tomorrow, John-boy," said his mum.

"I hate schools," moaned John. "I don't want another one."

"You're lucky to have a place," said
Mum. "You'll make friends there."

"I won't," said John.

Rosie was crying, and Mum started
singing to try and cheer her up. Dad
came in, wiping his feet and talking
to Uncle Levy. Billy turned up the
sound on the television.

John slipped out through the doorway. It was quiet outside, except for the cars driving past.

Pie stood tied to a rope that was pegged into the ground. John went up to her.

"Hey, my Pie lassie." John spoke softly. Pie nodded her big hard head and snorted warm breath. She tugged on her rope.

"Let's go and find some nice grass
for you," said John.

He untied the rope and pulled himself
up onto Pie's high wide back.

He clicked his tongue to make Pie go,
and they trotted down the lane through
the woods, away from the road.

John and Pie went through a dark
tunnel of trees that made shushing
sounds in the wind. They splashed over
a stream and out of the woods.

"Whoa."

They stopped. In front of them was
a big green field with a hedge full of
blackberries around the edge.

John told Pie, "I'll pick some
blackberries for Mum."

There was a smart brown pony
in the field. When the pony saw them,
his ears went back. He stood and
looked at Pie
and John.

"Hello," said John, and he clicked
his tongue.

Pie tossed her head and stamped.
John laughed. "Be nice, Pie!"

15

The brown pony came trotting up
to the gate, and John reached over and
stroked its nose. It was sleek and warm.
The pony blew friendly warm breath
on John's cold hands. "See?" said John
to Pie. "He's a friend."

Pie nudged her nose close to the
pony. John stroked both of them.
He looked at the big field full
of juicy green grass. Then he
slid down off Pie's back.
John pulled the gate
lever and swung
the gate open.
"Go on!" he told Pie.
"There's too much
for him to eat
on his own!"

The sun sank low in the sky and
turned pink behind the black trees.
Pie and the brown pony galloped
around the field, snorting together,
racing. John picked blackberries and
folded up his jumper to collect them in.
Then he stood and watched Pie and
the brown pony running together.

It was getting dark.

"Come, Pie!" called John, and she trotted over to him. The brown pony came too. "You've got to stay here," John told the pony. "But thank you for your grass."

John led Pie through the gate, then closed it behind them.

He climbed the gate to get onto
Pie's back without squashing
the blackberries.

They walked back through the dark
woods to the silver trailer with glowing
windows. Dad came out. He pegged
Pie's rope and gave her water.

"Food's ready," he said.

"I've got blackberries," said John.
"Good lad," said Dad. He opened
the trailer door and the light and
smells of cooking welcomed
John home.

Making Friends

*J*ohn walked slowly behind Billy,
looking at his feet. He could hear
schoolchildren shouting somewhere
down the road. Round the corner
he saw the school.

There was a fence all around it, and a big gate. John walked more slowly. He saw lots of children on the other side of the fence. The children stopped what they were doing and looked at John and Billy.

"Go on," said Billy. He pushed
John through the gate.
"Get off!" said John.

Billy pulled John up to the front door
and pressed a button. A buzzer went,
and Billy opened the door and made
John go through it. Inside, Billy went
up some stairs to his class. John had to
go into a different classroom.

30

"Hello, John!" said the teacher. Then she told the class, "This is John. He is joining us. There's an empty place over there, John."

John sat. Everyone looked
at John, but John didn't look at anyone.

The lesson was about animals.
The teacher wanted to know what
pets everybody had.

"Have you got a pet?"
she asked John.

John didn't answer.

"Perhaps you've got a cat?" said the teacher.

John shook his head.

"A guinea pig?"

John shook his head.

The teacher asked John, "Have you got *any* animals?"

"I might have," said John.

"Well," said the teacher. "I'm going to give everyone a piece of paper. I want you all to write down everything you can about one particular animal. You can make it up if you like."

The boy next to John wrote and wrote. John watched the boy's bit of paper turning dark with writing.

The boy looked at John and said,
"You've got to do writing too."
"I haven't," said John.

John picked up a pencil and began
to draw. He drew ears and then a line
that went down and round a nose and
under a cheek.

The boy stopped writing to watch
John draw.

John drew an eye. He drew a
wide strong body and knobbly legs
that ended in hooves. The legs were
galloping. John drew a tassel
of tail and
a ripple
of mane.

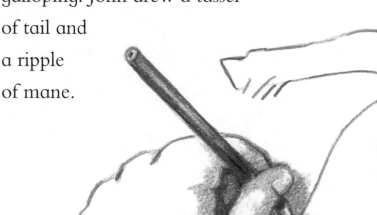

"Wow!" said the boy.
"Is that pony yours?"
"Yep," said John.

At playtime John stood by the gate
watching, hoping that Billy might join
him. But Billy was playing football
with the big boys.

"Hey!" said the writing boy.
"Tell me about your pony."
"Why?" asked John.

"I've got a pony too," said the boy.
"He's called Toffee and he's the best."
"Can't be the best," said John.
"Why not?"
"Pie's the best, so yours can't be."

"He can," argued the boy. "Toffee is a toffee-brown colour, but with white socks."

"Like you, you mean?" John looked at the boy's socks. Then he asked, "Does Toffee live in a field by a big house?"

"Yes," said the boy. "How d'you know that?"

"I've met him," said John. "Pie met him too. Pie can run faster than your horse."

The boy frowned at John. "Have you been in our field?"

John laughed.

"What's funny?" asked the boy.

"You look like your horse when he saw Pie," said John. "He was cross until they made friends."

"How d'you know they made friends?"

"They ran together."

"Oh, I wish I'd seen them." The boy smiled. "Will you bring Pie over sometime?"

"I might," said John. "Anyway, what's your name?"

"Tom," said the boy.

"Race you back to the classroom," shouted John as he began to run.

They ran really fast
across the playground
and into the school.
"Careful, boys!"
said their teacher.

They reached the classroom at
exactly the same time.

"I'm the fastest!"

"I am!"

Then they bent over and panted,
and they laughed.

Time to Go

seaside

school

Tom's house

mountains

church

John jumped out of the silver
trailer into a bright frosty morning.
Pie puffed misty breath in the cold.
"You off to school?" asked Dad.
He was lifting the harness over Pie's
head. A noisy lorry went past. "Not
much longer in this place, John-boy,
and then we're going near the
sea. You'll like that."

John kicked the trailer wheel. "But
I've got a friend here now. Tom lives
in that big house through the woods."

"We'll be back again one of these
days," said Dad.

John pulled up some
grass and offered it to Pie.
She snuffled and munched.

John banged a fist on the trailer door.
"Are you coming, Billy?"
Billy and John
ran all the way
to school.

In class they were doing different work now. It was a project about where they lived.

"Shush, everybody!" said their teacher. "Now, I want you to get into groups of two or three."

Tom asked John, "Will you make
a group with me?"

"Maybe," said John.

"I want you to work together to
draw a map that shows where you
live," said the teacher. "I want each
of you to draw your home on the map
and write something about it."

John frowned. "I hate writing."

"Well, I can't draw," said Tom. "So you do the drawing and I'll do the writing."

"But where do I draw? My home moves around."

"Then it'll have to be a big map," said Tom. "Bigger than all the others. It can show lots of your places, and my house, and the school, and loads of things. Come home with me and see my house, then you'll know how to draw it."

So after school, John told Billy to tell
Mum that he'd be home late.

John went back to Tom's house with
Tom and his mum and his sisters.

They had drinks and
biscuits in the kitchen.
Then Tom showed
John all the rooms.
Tom's bedroom
was at the top
of the house.

"That's my computer," said
Tom. But John was looking
out of the window.

"There's Toffee
in the field," he
said. "And look!
See the trees there?
See the smoke?
That's from
our trailer."

They went down to the field to see
Toffee and feed him old apples.

"Can you draw him?" asked Tom.

So John leaned his pad of paper on
the fence and drew Toffee. Then
he drew Tom's house.

"That's really good," said Tom.
"I can see my bedroom window!
I wish I could draw
like that."

At school the next day, they made their map. John drew Tom's house and their school. He drew the woods and the road that ran past their trailer. He drew other roads and mountains and towns and the seaside. Tom wrote what everything was.

school

seaside

church

"Draw your face, looking out of your bedroom window," said John.

So Tom did.

John made a trailer out of a small box. He covered it in silver foil and stuck on cardboard wheels and paper windows. He drew himself looking out of the window. The trailer could move around the map.

"What about Toffee and Pie?" asked Tom.

"We can make them out of cardboard," said John. "They can have wool tails."

"Put them in the field," said Tom. "Then they can run together."

"That's excellent work, boys," said the teacher when she saw their finished map. "Well done, both of you."

After school, John took Pie over to Tom's. They rode Pie and Toffee in the field.

"We're moving on soon," John told Tom.

"Why?"

"That's what we do," said John.
"We'll come back again. Maybe next
blackberry time. You keep our map,"
he added. "I'll remember where
your house is."

"OK," said Tom. "Thanks."

Then they had
a last gallop together
as the sun went down.